D0396663

♡ The Wildwood Bakery ♡

Read more OWL DIARIES books!
1
OWL DIARIES
Eva's Treetop Festival
Rebecca Elliott
2
OWL DIARIES
Eva Sees a Ghost
Rebecca Elliott
3
OWL DIARIES
A Woodland Wedding
Rebecca Elliott
4
OWL DIARIES
Eva and the New Owl
Rebecca Elliott
5
OWL DIARIES
Warm Hearts Day
Rebecca Elliott
6
OWL DIARIES
Buster is Missing
Rebecca Elliott
7
OWL DIARIES
The Wildwood Bakery
Rebecca Elliott
8
OWL DIARIES
Eva and the Lost Pony
Rebecca Elliott

Elliott, Rebecca,
The Wildwood Bakery /
[2017]
33305240222541
wo 11/16/17

For Maisy and Katie, who have the coolest wingchairs around.—R.E.

Special thanks to Eva Montgomery.

If you purchased this book without a cover, you should be aware that this book is stolen property. It was reported as "unsold and destroyed" to the publisher, and neither the author nor the publisher has received any payment for this "stripped book."

Copyright © 2017 by Rebecca Elliott

All rights reserved. Published by Scholastic Inc., *Publishers since 1920.* SCHOLASTIC, BRANCHES, and associated logos are trademarks and/or registered trademarks of Scholastic Inc.

The publisher does not have any control over and does not assume any responsibility for author or third-party websites or their content.

No part of this publication may be reproduced, stored in a retrieval system, or transmitted in any form or by any means, electronic, mechanical, photocopying, recording, or otherwise, without written permission of the publisher. For information regarding permission, write to Scholastic Inc., Attention: Permissions Department, 557 Broadway, New York, NY 10012.

This book is a work of fiction. Names, characters, places, and incidents are either the product of the author's imagination or are used fictitiously, and any resemblance to actual persons, living or dead, business establishments, events, or locales is entirely coincidental.

Library of Congress Cataloging-in-Publication Data
Names: Elliott, Rebecca, author. | Elliott, Rebecca. Owl diaries ; 7.
Title: The Wildwood Bakery / Rebecca Elliott.
Description: First edition. | New York : Branches/Scholastic Inc., 2017. |
Series: Owl diaries ; 7 | Summary: Macy's little sister has wings that are too small, so Eva's class decides to raise money to buy her a flying chair, and half the class opens a bakery, and the other half opens a candy store—but soon competition between the two stores becomes more important than their goal, and Eva needs to convince the other owls that they will collect more money if everyone works as a team.
Identifiers: LCCN 2017015799 | ISBN 9781338163001 (pbk.) | ISBN 9781338163018 (hardcover)
Subjects: LCSH: Owls—Juvenile fiction. | Elementary schools—Juvenile fiction. | Money-making projects for children—Juvenile fiction. | Bakeries—Juvenile fiction. | Cooperativeness—Juvenile fiction. | Diaries—Juvenile fiction. | CYAC: Owls—Fiction. | Schools—Fiction. | Fund raising—Fiction. | Bakers and bakeries—Fiction. | Cooperativeness—Fiction. | Diaries—Fiction.
Classification: LCC PZ7.E45812 Wi 2017 | DDC [Fic]—dc23 LC record available at https://lccn.loc.gov/2017015799

10 9 8 7 6 5 4 3 2 1 17 18 19 20 21

Printed in China 38
First edition, November 2017

Book design by Marissa Asuncion
Edited by Katie Carella

Table of Contents

1 Well, Hello There! 1
2 The Wingchair Plan 12
3 Yummy Scrummy 20
4 Granny to the Rescue! 28
5 Ninja Carrot Hunters 40
6 Emergency Meeting 49
7 Cupcakes vs. Candy 56
8 The Wingball Champion! 68

11
Woodpine Avenue

1

♡ Well, Hello There! ♡

Sunday

Hello Diary,

Did you miss me? It's me – Eva Wingdale! I wonder what exciting adventure we'll have this week!

I love:

Granny Owlberta's cookies

The word bubble

Saving up my moon dollars

Funny jokes

Squirrels

Baby Mo's laugh

Helping others

Winning at **WINGBALL**

I DO NOT love:

Stinky cheese

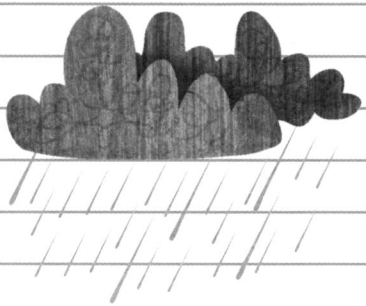

Rain clouds

Baby Mo's cry

Cleaning my room

Washing my wings before I eat

The word gray

Mom's slug stew

Losing at **WINGBALL**

My family is **FLAPERIFFIC**!

Here is a picture of us on Warm Hearts Day:

We all love Baxter – my cute pet bat.

I'm so lucky to be an owl. Owls do the best stuff . . .

We are awake when the sun has gone to bed.

We fly like superheroes.

We make super loud hoot sounds.

And we hatch out of eggs when we're chicks!

This is my tree house.
11
I live next door to my best friend EVER, Lucy Beakman. We sit together in Mrs. Featherbottom's class.
9

Here is our class photo:

I can't wait to see all my friends at school tomorrow! Better get some sleep. Good day, Diary!

2

♡The Wingchair Plan♡

Monday

Today, Mrs. Featherbottom asked us each to share something we did over the weekend.

I sewed a new dress – with my mom's help.
I took photos of the sunset.
I visited my big brother in Owlahoma City.

I ate at an Owltalian restaurant.
I went to the featherdresser!
I made a flower fairy costume for my pet lizard, Rex.
I baked my dad a birthday cake.

OWL NINJA
REBECCA SCHIDDT
I read the new Owl Ninja book.
I practiced playing my owlaphone.
I went to Brown Bear Mall with my little sister, Mia. We bought her a school bag.

Wow, Macy! I didn't know your sister was starting school.
Mia's starting preschool next week. She can't wait! She's worried though, because she can't fly like everyone else. She was born with wings that are too small.
Why doesn't she have a wingchair to help her get around?
They're very expensive. Mom and Dad just don't have enough moon dollars.

Just then, I had a **FLAP-TASTIC** idea!

After school, Lucy came over, and we baked cookies.

Then I had ANOTHER **FLAP-TASTIC** IDEA – and so did Lucy! Both at the same time!

I'm SO excited! I can't wait to tell everyone our idea tomorrow!

3

Yummy Scrummy

Tuesday

School was such a **HOOT** today, Diary! Mrs. Featherbottom asked us to share our fund-raising ideas.

A pet salon!
A sweet shop!
A teacher-dunking booth!
A photo booth!
A costume party!
A tree house window-cleaning service!
A bakery!

Wow! These are all EGG-CELLENT! It's hard to pick just one. So, I'm going to pick two! And it might be because I'm hungry, but I choose Sue's sweet shop idea AND Eva and Lucy's bakery idea!
Yay!

This half of the class will join Sue's group, and that half will join Eva and Lucy's group. You'll spend the week getting your shops ready!
Both shops will be at the Old Oak Tree, and they'll be open Saturday and Sunday. Together, we'll raise the money Mia needs in no time!
We all cheered.

At lunch, we sat in our groups.

It took us AGES to come up with a name . . .

We all LOVED Macy's idea.

Hey, I heard Sue's team is having a secret meeting right now!
If they're holding secret meetings, then we will, too!
We should have a secret password.
Yes! What should it be?
How about yummy scrummy?
That's great!

Next, we made a list of everything we need to do before Saturday:

After school, we went to my tree house to bake. But the cookie batter didn't taste good. So we used it for a food fight instead!

We'll have to bake FOR REAL tomorrow . . .

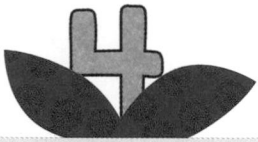

♡ Granny to the Rescue! ♡

Wednesday

Diary, sometimes Sue can be nice and sometimes Sue can be, well, Sue. Today, Sue was being Sue.

During class, both teams worked on shop signs. Zac came up with ours.

We copied it to make our Wildwood Bakers membership cards.

At recess, I called our first secret Wildwood Bakers meeting. Everyone showed their cards and said the password. It was such a **HOOT**!

Everyone looked at me like I was crazy.

Later, we told Granny Owlberta and Grandpa Owlfred about our shop.

We baked YUMMY cookies.

Then Hailey thought she saw someone at the window.

We flew outside.

No one was there. But Macy found something.
Hey, look at this!
It's a membership card!
Candy Crunch Corner
Someone from Candy Crunch Corner was here!
They must be spying on us!

We flew back inside.

Granny is a very wise old owl. In order to do our BEST though, we'll need more than a cookie recipe.

Granny, do you have a really great cupcake recipe?
I have one that is very special.
She took a dusty recipe book down from a shelf.
This is an old Wingdale Family recipe. These Dreamy Creamy Carrot Cupcakes are so good, it is impossible to eat just one.
Legend has it that your Great-Great-Grandpa Wingston once ate so many Dreamy Creamies that he couldn't fly for a month!

Dreamy Creamy Carrot Cupcakes

1 cup sugar
1 cup flour
6 bugs
2 acorns
1 cup wild carrots

- Mix together the first 4 ingredients
- Shred the carrots and stir them in
- Pour batter into muffin pan
- Bake for 30 minutes
- Let cupcakes cool
- Put loads of icing on top
- Enjoy!

Those cupcakes sound yummy!
Can we bake them now?
I'm afraid not. I don't have any wild carrots. They are hard to find!
Oh.

Then Granny whispered:

Everyone said good-bye to Granny and Grandpa. Then we all flew home.

Diary, tomorrow we are going to find those wild carrots and bake those Dreamy Creamies! It's the ONLY way we'll win.

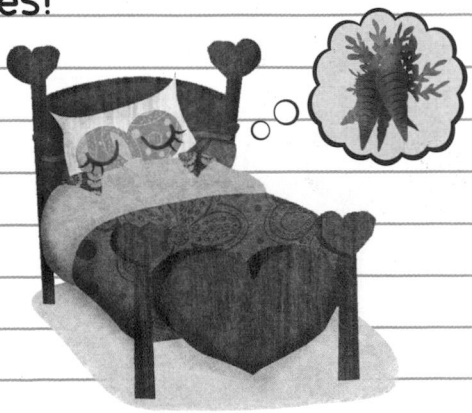

5

♡ Ninja Carrot Hunters ♡

Thursday

When we got to school, everyone was whispering about secret plans for the shops. Sue was listening in on us. Again. It made me a bit mad.

Mrs. Featherbottom called Sue and me over to her desk.

I knew Mrs. Featherbottom was right. But I also still REALLY wanted our shop to raise more money than Sue's.

I called another secret Wildwood Bakers meeting.

When the Wildwood Bakers met up, we all looked so cool!

We flew around the forest looking for a rabbit.

We followed the rabbit to a patch of wild carrots. We hid in a tree and kept really quiet.
What now? Do we just take their carrots?
Those are wild carrots — they don't belong to the rabbits.
But still . . . We should ask before taking them.
I'll go talk to the rabbits. Wait here.

Excuse me. My friends and I would like to pick your wild carrots to bake some cupcakes. Is that okay?
Sure.
Thank you!
We're actually bored of eating carrots. It's all we ever eat. Plain carrots. All day long.
What if I bring you some carrot cupcakes?
That sounds yummy. Thank you!

My friends flew down, and we picked wild carrots together.

Back at my tree house, we baked the Dreamy Creamies.

We baked SO MANY that we used up all our sugar!

Dad was our first taste tester.

Diary, my bedroom is FILLED with cookies and cupcakes. YUM!

6

Emergency Meeting

Friday

Hi Diary,

I cannot believe it's already Friday! Our shop opens tomorrow!!

At recess today, we had fun playing **WINGBALL**. But the nets, uniforms, and balls are so old they're falling apart.

Can Mia play wingball?
Well, she can't fly so she can't really play. . . But she is great at catching the ball.
After Mia gets her wingchair, she'll be able to play!
You're right! That would make her so happy. Do you really think our shops will make enough moon dollars for a wingchair?
They have to. For Mia!

Just then, Sue's team flew over.

Then Sue said:

We passed out flyers, but we haven't seen any of yours. You'll be lucky if you get one customer!

ARGHHHHH!!!

Oh no! We should've made our flyers days ago!!

I called an emergency meeting at lunchtime. We looked at our to-do list:

1. Design our shop sign
2. Make flyers to advertise the shop
3. Bake cookies to sell and cupcakes
4. Decorate shop bags
5. Make garlands for inside the shop

There's still so much to do!

How did we forget about the flyers? Now no one knows about our shop!

Don't worry. We'll get it all done. Let's meet after school. Okay?

My little sister, Mia, wants to help. Can she come?

Of course! We need all the helping wings we can get!

After school, we worked hard.

Lucy and I made the garlands.

Zac and Hailey made the flyers.

George, Macy, and Mia decorated the bags. (We were lucky Mia helped out!)

We got everything ready in no time.

Next, we flew around the forest. We left a flyer on every doorstep so EVERYONE would know about our shop.

I can't wait for tomorrow!

7

Cupcakes vs. Candy

Saturday

We flew to the Old Oak Tree super early. We decorated our shop and put out the cupcakes and cookies.

Customers were lined up outside. Our families and friends and neighbors were all there!

Finally, it was time to open the shop.

Oh my, Diary! Running a bakery is hard work . . .

We had to get the cupcakes and cookies for everyone.

We had to bag them up.

And we had to charge the right amount of moon dollars.

I took a quick peek at Candy Crunch Corner. Sue's shop seemed to have just as many owls in it as ours. So I wasn't sure who was winning.

At the end of the night, we were closing up when . . .

We've run out of cupcakes and cookies!
We don't have anything to sell tomorrow?!
That means Sue's team will win!
Not if we bake more cupcakes and cookies tonight!
But we don't have any sugar left. And the grocery store is closed!
Secret meeting – NOW!
THE WILDWOOD BAKERY

We huddled together.

Everyone was quiet. We were all thinking hard about this decision.

We flew to Candy Crunch Corner. Sue's team was all in a **FLAP** – just like we were!

Candy Crunch Corner
We've run out of bags! What are we going to do!?
We can't pack up our candies without bags!
We'll never win now!
What if we ask Eva and Lucy's team for bags?
No way! We can't ask them for help!

Just then, we heard Mia's voice behind us.

I don't think I want a wingchair anymore. I thought these shops were supposed to be a fun way to help me. But the two teams aren't even friends anymore, and all you guys seem to want to do is win.

Everyone felt bad. We had forgotten why we were doing this in the first place. We had also forgotten we were all friends. And friends help one another.

Sorry we tried so hard to win, Sue. Your shop really does look flap-tastic.
Sorry we spied on your team, Eva. Your cupcakes look super yummy.
I have an idea! Your shop needs bags, and our shop needs sugar. Let's join together to make one super-sugary-sweet candy bake shop!
That's a flappy-fabulous idea, Macy!

Mrs. Featherbottom came to see how our shops had done in their first night. She counted up the moon dollars.

Mia and her Dad flew off.

We told Mrs. Featherbottom our plan to put both shops together. She loved it!

We all flew to Sue's house to bake. We had a **FLAPERRIFIC** time!

When I got home, Humphrey burst into my room.

How's the bakery, Eva? Save any treats for me?

I did actually. Here you go.

Oh no!

What is it?

I forgot to take cupcakes to the rabbits who gave us the carrots!

So, Diary, I've set my alarm for super early tomorrow. I'm so tired . . .

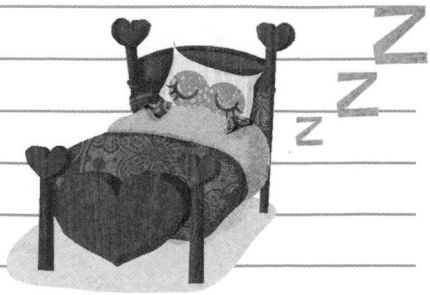

The Wingball Champion!

Sunday

I flew to the rabbits' carrot patch when it was still light.

Thank you so much for helping us. Here are cupcakes just for you.

Wow, these are hopperrific!

Really yummy!

The new Wildcandy Cake Shop was a big success tonight! We had so much fun working together! After we closed up our shop, we ate the leftover treats.

Then Mia flew – yes, FLEW – in on her new wingchair!

Check out my new, totally owlsome wings! I cannot wait for my first day of school tomorrow!
THE WILDCANDY CAKE SHOP
We're happy we could help!

I'm so proud of all of you. And . . . Surprise! The school is going to use the money you raised tonight to buy new wingball nets, balls, and uniforms!
I bought one new ball already! Mia, catch!
The ball flew through the air.

Mia swooped up to catch it. She moved faster than any owl I've ever seen!

We all cheered! This was such a great week, Diary. See you next time!

Rebecca Elliott was a lot like Eva when she was younger: She loved making things and hanging out with her best friends. Now that Rebecca is older, not much has changed — except that her best friends are her husband, Matthew, and their children. She still loves making things, like stories, cakes, music, and paintings. But as much as she and Eva have in common, Rebecca cannot fly or turn her head all the way around. No matter how hard she tries.

Rebecca is the author of JUST BECAUSE and MR. SUPER POOPY PANTS. OWL DIARIES is her first early chapter book series.

OWL DIARIES

How much do you know about The Wildwood Bakery?

What is a wingchair? How is it similar to a wheelchair? Why does Mia need one?

Look at page 43. Why are the Wildwood Bakers dressed like ninjas?

What is the disaster that happens at the end of the Wildwood Bakery's first night?

Mia uses a special wingchair to fly. Do you know anyone who uses something special to help them?

How is the Wildcandy Cake Shop formed? Use details to describe the thoughts, feelings, and actions of Eva and her classmates.